DINOSAURS

Look and Find®

pi kids®

publications international, ltd.

Greetings! My name is Doctor Zeen, paleontologist. That means I study dinosaurs. Welcome to my Dinosaur Museum! I have been working on this project for more than a year. Join the tour and let's look for these dinosaurs.

Othnielia

Tuojiangosaurus

Stegosaurus

Brachiosaurus

Apatosaurus

Allosaurus

GRAND

This next exhibit features the carnivorous dinosaurs of the late Cretaceous. These dinosaurs ate meat, including other dinosaurs. Can you find these appetizing carnivorous-dinosaur snacks?

Hypacrosaurus

Troodon

Albertosaurus

Dromaeosaurus

Tyrannosaurus rex

Protoceratops

There was a lot of marine life in the dinosaur age. Many of these creatures still have relatives living today, like crocodiles and starfish. Can you find these aquatic animals?

Mosasaurus

Ichthyosaurus

Deinosuchus

Hesperornis

Globidens

Plesiosaurus

In this exhibit we have our herbivores. They only eat plants. Many herbivores had horns or spikes to protect themselves. Can you find these dinosaurs?

Shantungosaurus

Brachyceratops

Ankylosaurus

Kritosaurus

Corythosaurus

Edmontosaurus

As you can see, dinosaurs laid eggs much like lizards, snakes, and other reptiles. Some dinosaurs guarded over their young until they were able to take care of themselves. See if you can find these baby dinosaurs.

Torosaurus

Pachycephalosaurus

Centrosaurus

Bactrosaurus

Panoplosaurus

Leptoceratops

The word *dinosaur* refers only to land-dwelling prehistoric lizards that stand upright. Pterosaurs don't fit this definition, but they are dinosaur relatives and have many similarities, such as being reptiles and laying eggs. Can you find all of these pterosaurs?

This pterosaur egg

Baby *Caulkicephalus*

Coloborhynchus

Caulkicephalus

This *Pteranodon*

This *Pteranodon*

There are many theories as to what caused the mass dinosaur extinction, such as a meteorite impact, starvation, and change of climate. If you look closely you'll see some animals that survived the mass extinction.

Eomaia

Lizard

Frog

Turtle

Salamander

Snakes

This is where the magic happens! Paleontologists study dinosaur fossils to learn more about these giant reptiles. Everything we know and every exhibit we have created started right here!

Torosaurus horn

Tyrannosaurus rex jaw

Pteranodon wing bone

Ankylosaurus spike

Stegosaurus back plate

Plesiosaurus fin

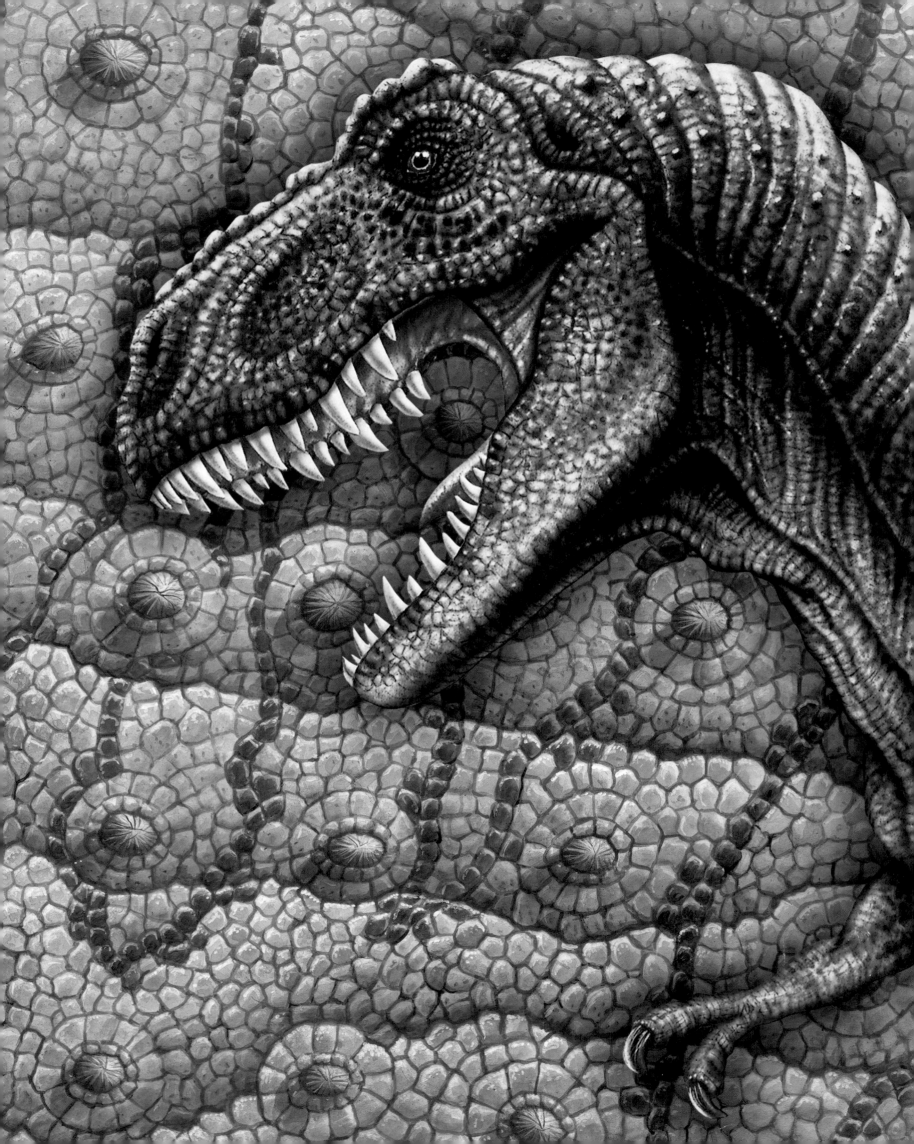